W9-BCS-826

P 0.5

Dear Parent:

Congratulations! Your child is taking the first steps on an exciting journey. The destination? Independent reading!

STEP INTO READING® will help your child get there. The program offers five steps to reading success. Each step includes fun stories and colorful art. There are also Step into Reading Sticker Books, Step into Reading Math Readers, Step into Reading Write-In Readers, Step into Reading Phonics Readers, and Step into Reading Phonics First Steps! Boxed Sets—a complete literacy program with something for every child.

Learning to Read, Step by Step!

Ready to Read Preschool–Kindergarten
• big type and easy words • rhyme and rhythm • picture clues
For children who know the alphabet and are eager to begin reading.

Reading with Help Preschool–Grade 1
• basic vocabulary • short sentences • simple stories
For children who recognize familiar words and sound out new words with help.

Reading on Your Own Grades 1–3
• engaging characters • easy-to-follow plots • popular topics
For children who are ready to read on their own.

Reading Paragraphs Grades 2–3
• challenging vocabulary • short paragraphs • exciting stories
For newly independent readers who read simple sentences with confidence.

Ready for Chapters Grades 2–4
• chapters • longer paragraphs • full-color art
For children who want to take the plunge into chapter books but still like colorful pictures.

STEP INTO READING® is designed to give every child a successful reading experience. The grade levels are only guides. Children can progress through the steps at their own speed, developing confidence in their reading, no matter what their grade.

Remember, a lifetime love of reading starts with a single step!

For Mookie—L.D.

Visit us on the Web!
www.stepintoreading.com
www.randomhouse.com/kids/disney

Educators and librarians, for a variety of teaching tools, visit us at
www.randomhouse.com/teachers

Library of Congress Cataloging-in-Publication Data
Driscoll, Laura.
Smash trash! / by Laura Driscoll. — 1st ed.
    p. cm. — (Step into reading. Step 1 book)
Summary: As his pet cockroach keeps him company, WALL•E the robot shovels and scoops trash into his compacter every day, creating compacted trash blocks, and finding "goodies" to collect.
ISBN 978-0-7364-2515-5 — ISBN 978-0-7364-8058-1 (Gibraltar lib. ed.)
[1. Refuse and refuse disposal—Fiction. 2. Robots—Fiction. 3. Cockroaches—Fiction.]
I. Title.
PZ7.D79Sm 2008   [E]—dc22   2007041593

Printed in the United States of America   10 9 8 7 6 5 4 3 2 1   First Edition

Disney · PIXAR

WALL·E

SMASH TRASH!

By Laura Driscoll
Illustrated by Mario Cortes
Painted by Giorgio Vallorani
Inspired by the art and character designs created by Pixar

Random House New York

WALL•E is a robot.

He lives around trash.

Trash here.

Trash there.

Trash everywhere.

It is one big mess.

The sun gives
WALL•E power.

Off to work!

Scoop the trash.

Trash goes in.

Smash!

Smash trash.

Stack trash.

Smash trash.

Smash more trash.

Ooooh!

A goody!

Smash trash.

Keep the goody.

One more goody!

This goody is messy!

Save the goodies.

Smash trash.

WALL•E heads home
with his new goodies.

Oh, no!

His alarm flashes.

A dust storm comes.

WALL•E cubes up.

The storm passes.

WALL•E uncubes.

He rolls home.

WALL·E takes off
his treads.

He puts

his new goodies away.

This one here.

That one there.

Everything is just so.

Bedtime!

WALL·E cubes up.

He shuts down.

It is a new day.

Smash more trash!